THE TALE OF HOGNI AND HEDINN

THE TALE OF HOGNI AND HEDINN

translated by

EIRIKR MAGNUSSON AND
WILLIAM MORRIS

WILDSIDE PRESS

COPYRIGHT INFORMATION

Published by Wildside Press LLC.
www.wildsidebooks.com

CHAPTER I

OF FREYIA AND THE DWARFS

East of Vanaquisl in Asia was the land called Asialand or Asiahome, but the folk that dwelt there was called Aesir, and their chief town was Asgard. Odin was the name of the king thereof, and therein was a right holy place of sacrifice. Niord and Frey Odin made Temple-priests thereover; but the daughter of Niord was Freyia, and she was fellow to Odin and his concubine.

Now there were certain men in Asia, whereof one was called Alfrigg, the second Dwalin, the third Berling, the fourth Grerr: these had their abode but a little space from the King's hall, and were men so wise in craftsmanship, that they laid skilful hand on all matters; and such-like men as they were did men call dwarfs. In a rock was their dwelling, and in that day they mingled more with menfolk than as now they do.

Odin loved Freyia full sore, and withal she was the fairest woman of that day: she had a bower that was both fair and strong; insomuch, say men, that if the door were shut to, none might come into the bower aforesaid without the will of Freyia.

Now on a day went Freyia afoot by that rock of the dwarfs, and it lay open: therein were the dwarfs a-smithying a golden collar, and the work was at point to be done: fair seemed that collar to Freyia, and fair seemed Freyia to the dwarfs.

Now would Freyia buy the collar of them, and bade them in return for it silver and gold, and other good things. They said they lacked not money, yet that each of them would sell his share of the collar for this thing, and for nought else—that she should lie a night by each of them: wherefore, whether she liked it better or worse, on such wise did she strike the bargain with them; and so the four nights being outworn, and all conditions fulfilled, they delivered the collar to Freyia; and she went home to her bower, and held her peace hereof, as if nought had befallen.

CHAPTER II

OF THE STEALING OF FREYIA'S COLLAR, AND HOW SHE MAY HAVE IT AGAIN

There was a man called Farbauti, which carl had to wife a carline called Laufey; she was both slim and slender, therefore was she called Needle. One child had these, a son called Loki; nought great of growth was he, but betimes shameless of tongue and nimble in gait; over all men had he that craft which is called cunning; guileful was he from his youth up, therefore was he called Loki the Sly.

He betook himself to Odin at Asgard and became his man. Ever had Odin a good word for him, whatsoever he turned to; yet withal he oft laid heavy labours upon him, which forsooth he turned out of hand better than any man looked for: moreover, he knew wellnigh all things that befell, and told all he knew to Odin.

So tells the tale that Loki knew how that Freyia had gotten the collar, yea, and what she had given for it; so he told Odin thereof, and when Odin heard of it he bade Loki get the collar and bring it to him. Loki said it was not a likely business, because no man might come into Freyia's bower without the will of her; but Odin bade him go his ways and not come back before he had gotten the collar. Then Loki turned away howling, and most of men were glad thereof whenas Loki throve nought.

But Loki went to Freyia's bower, and it was locked; he strove to come in, and might not; and cold it was without, so that he fast began to grow a-cold.

So he turned himself into a fly, and fluttered about all the locks and the joints, and found no hole therein whereby he might come in, till up by the gable-top he found a hole, yet no bigger than one might thrust a needle through; none the less he wriggled in thereby. So when he was come in he peered all about to see if any waked, but soon he got to see that all were asleep in the bower. Then in he goeth unto Freyia's bed, and sees that she hath the collar on her with the clasp turned downward.

Thereon Loki changed himself into a flea, and sat on Freyia's cheek, and stung her so that she woke and turned about, and then fell asleep again.

Then Loki drew from off him his flea's shape, and un-did the collar, and opened the bower, and gat him gone to Odin therewith.

Next morn awoke Freyia and saw that the doors were open, yet unbroken, and that the goodly collar was gone. She deemed she knew what guile had wrought it, so she goeth into the hall when she is clad, and cometh before Odin the king, and speaketh to him of the evil he has let be wrought against her in the stealing of that dear thing, and biddeth him give her back her jewel.

Odin says that in such wise hath she gotten it, that never again shall she have it. "Unless forsooth thou bring to pass, that two kings, each served of twenty kings, fall to strife, and fight under such weird and spell, that they no sooner fall adown than they stand up again and fight on: always unless some christened man be so bold of heart, and the fate and fortune of his lord be so great, that he shall dare go into that battle, and smite with weapons these men: and so first shall their toil come to an end, to whatsoever lord it shall befall to loose them from the pine and trouble of their fell deeds."

Hereto said Freyia yea, and gat her collar again.

CHAPTER III

OF KING ERLING, AND SORLI HIS SON

In those days, when four-and-twenty winters were worn away from the death of Peace-Frodi, a king ruled over the Uplands in Norway called Erling. He had a queen and two sons; Sorli the Strong the elder, and Erlend the younger: hopeful were they both, but Sorli was the stronger. They fell to warfare so soon as they were of age thereto; they fought with the viking Sindri, son of Sveigr, the son of Haki, the sea-king, at the Elfskerries; and there fell the viking Sindri and all his folk; there also fell Erlend Erlingson. Thereafter Sorli sailed into the East-salt-sea, and harried there, and did so many doughty deeds that late it were ere all were written down.

CHAPTER IV

SORLI SLAYETH KING HALFDAN

There was a king hight Halfdan, who ruled over Denmark, and abode in a stead called Roi's-well; he had to wife Hvedna the old, and their sons were Hogni and Hakon, men peerless of growth and might, and all prowess: they betook them to warfare so soon as they were come to man's estate.

Now cometh the tale on Sorli again, for on an autumn-tide he sailed to Denmark. King Halfdan was minded as at this time to go to an assembly of the kings; he was well stricken in years when these things betid. He had a dragon so good that never was such another ship in all Norway for strength's sake, and all craftsmanship. Now was this ship lying moored in the haven, but King Halfdan was a-land and had let brew his farewell drink. But when Sorli saw the dragon, so great covetise ran into his heart that he must needs have her: and forsooth, as most men say, no ship so goodly hath been in the Northlands, but it were the dragon Ellida, or Gnod, or the Long Worm.

So Sorli spake to his men, bidding them array them for battle; "for we will slay King Halfdan and have away his dragon."

Then answered his word a man called Saevar, his Forecastle-man and Marshal: "Ill rede, lord," saith he; "for King Halfdan is a mighty lord of great renown, and hath two sons to avenge him, who are either of them full famous men.

"Let them be mightier than the very Gods," said Sorli, "yet shall I none the less join battle."

So they arrayed them for the fight.

Now came tidings hereof to King Halfdan, and he started up and fared down to the ships with his men, and they got them ready for battle.

Some men set before King Halfdan that it was ill rede to fight, and it were best to flee away because of the odds; but the king said that they should fall every one across the other's feet or ever he should flee. So either side arrayed them, and joined battle of the fiercest; the end whereof was such that King Halfdan fell and all his folk, and Sorli took his dragon and all that was of worth.

Thereafter heard Sorli that Hogni was come from warfare, and lay by Odins-isle; so thitherward straight stood Sorli, and when they met he told him of the fall of Halfdan his father, and offered him atonement and self-doom, and they to become foster-brethren. But Hogni gainsayed him utterly: so they fought as it sayeth in Sorli's Song. Hakon went forth full fairly, and slew Saevar, Sorli's Banner-bearer and Forecastle-man, and therewith Sorli slew Hakon, and Hogni slew Erling the king, Sorli's father.

Then they fought together, Hogni and Sorli, and Sorli fell before Hogni for wounds and weariness' sake: but Hogni let heal him, and they swore the oath of brotherhood thereafter, and held it well whiles they both lived. Sorli was the shortest-lived of them; he fell in the East-sea before the vikings, as it saith in the Sorli-Song, and here saith:

Fell there the fight-greedy,

Foremost of war-host,
Eager in East-seas,
All on Hells' hall-floor;
Died there the doughty
In dale-fishes joy-tide,
With byrny-rod biting
The vikings in brand-thing.

But when Hogni heard of the fall of Sorli, he went a warring in the Eastlands that same summer, and had the victory in every place, and became king thereover; and so say men that twenty kings paid tribute to King Hogni, and held their realms of him.

Hogni won so great fame from his doughty deeds and his warfare that he was as well known by name north in the Finn-steads, as right away in Paris-town; yea, and all betwixt and between.

CHAPTER V

HEDINN HEARETH TELL OF
KING HOGNI, AND COMETH
TO THE NORTHLANDS

Hiarandi was the name of a king who ruled over Serkland; a queen he had, and one son named Hedinn, who from his youth up was peerless of growth, and strength, and prowess: from his early days he betook him to warfare, and became a Sea-king, and harried wide about Spain and the land of the Greeks, and all realms thereabout, till twenty kings paid tribute to him, and held of him land and fief.

On a winter abode Hedinn at home in Serkland, and it is said that on a time he went into the wood with his household; and so it befell him to be alone of his men in a certain wood-lawn, and there in the wood-lawn he saw a woman sitting on a chair, great of growth and goodly of aspect: he asked her of her name, and she named herself Gondul.

Then fell they a-talking, and she asked him of his doughty deeds, and lightly he told her all, and asked her if she wotted of any king who was his peer in daring and hardihood, in fame and furtherance; and she said she wotted of one who fell nowise short of him, and who was served of twenty kings no less than he, and that his name was Hogni, and his dwelling north in Denmark.

"Then wot I," said Hedinn, "that we shall try it which of us twain is foremost."

"Now will it be time for thee to go to thy men," said Gondul; "they will be seeking thee."

So they departed and he fared to his men, but she was left sitting there.

But so soon as spring was come Hedinn arrayed his departure, and had a dragon and three hundred men thereon: he made for the Northlands, and sailed all that summer and winter, and came to Denmark in the Springtide.

CHAPTER VI

HOGNI AND HEDINN MEET, AND SWEAR BROTHERHOOD TO EACH OTHER

King Hogni sat at home this while, and when he heard tell how a noble king is come to his land he bade him home to a glorious feast, and that Hedinn took. And as they sat at the drink, Hogni asked what errand Hedinn had thither, that had driven him so far north in the world.

Hedinn said that this was his errand, that they twain should try their hardihood and daring, their prowess and all their craftsmanship; and Hogni said he was all ready thereto.

So betimes on the morrow fared they to swimming and shooting at marks, and strove in tilting and fencing and all prowess; and in all skill were they so alike that none thought he could see betwixt them which was the foremost. Thereafter they swore themselves foster-brethren, and should halve all things between them.

Hedinn was young and unwedded, but Hogni was somewhat older, and he had to wife Hervor, daughter of Hiorvard, who was the son of Heidrek, who was the son of Wolfskin.

Hogni had a daughter, Hild by name, the fairest and wisest of all women, and he loved his daughter much. No other child had he.

CHAPTER VII

THE BEGUILING OF HEDINN,
AND OF HIS EVIL DEED

The tale telleth that Hogni went a-warring a little here-after, and left Hedinn behind to ward the realm. So on a day went Hedinn into the wood for his disport, and blithe was the weather. And yet again he turned away from his men and came into a certain wood-lawn, and there in the lawn beheld the same woman sitting in a chair, whom he had seen aforetime in Serkland, and him seemed that she was now gotten fairer than aforetime.

Yet again she first cast a word at him, and became kind in speech to him; she held a horn in her hand shut in with a lid, and the king's heart yearned toward her.

She bade the king drink, and he was thirsty, for he was gotten warm; so he took the horn and drank, and when he had drunk, lo a marvellous change came over him, for he remembered nought of all that was betid to him aforetime, and he sat him down and talked with her. She asked whether he had tried, as she had bidden him, the prowess of Hogni and his hardihood.

Hedinn said that sooth it was: "For he fell short of me in nought in any mastery we tried: so now are we called equal."

"Yet are ye nought equal," said she.

"Whereby makest thou that?" said he.

"In this wise," said she; "that Hogni hath a queen of high kindred, but thou hast no wife."

He answers: "Hogni will give me Hild, his daughter, so soon as I ask her; and then am I no worse wedded than he."

"Minished were thy glory then," she said, "wert thou to crave Hogni of alliance. Better were it, if forsooth thou lack neither hardihood nor daring according to thy boast, that thou have away Hild, and slay the Queen in this wise: to wit, to lay her down before the beak of that dragon ship, and let smite her asunder therewith in the launching of it."

Now so was Hedinn ensnared by evil heart and forgetfulness, because of the drink he had drunken, that nought seemed good to him save this; and he clean forgat that he and Hogni were foster-brethren.

So they departed, and Hedinn fared to his men and this befell when summer was far spent.

Now Hedinn ordained his men for the arraying of the dragon, saying that he would away for Serkland. Then went he to the bower, and took Hild and the queen, one by either hand, and went forth with them; and his men took Hild's raiment and fair things. Those men only were in the realm, who durst do nought for Hedinn and his men; for full fearful of countenance was he.

But Hild asked Hedinn what he would, and he told her; and she bade him do it not: "For," quoth she, "my father will give me to thee if thou woo me of him."

"I will not do so much as to woo thee," said Hedinn.

"And though," said she, "thou wilt do no otherwise than bear me away, yet may my father be appeased thereof: but if thou do this evil deed and unmanly, doing my mother to death, then never may my father be appeased:

and this wise have my dreams pointed, that ye shall fight and lay each other a-low; and then shall yet heavier things fall upon you: and great sorrow shall it be to me, if such a fate must fall upon my father that he must bear a dreadful weird and heavy spells: nor have I any joy to see thee sore-hearted under bitter toll."

Hedinn said he heeded nought what should come after, and that he would do his deed none the less.

"Yea, thou mayest none other do," said Hild, "for not of thyself dost thou it."

Then went Hedinn down to the strand, and the dragon was thrust forth, and the queen laid down before the beak thereof; and there she lost her life.

So went Hedinn aboard the dragon: but when all was dight he would fain go a-land alone of his men, and into the self-same wood wherein he had gone aforetime: and so, when he was come into the wood-lawn, there saw he Gondul sitting in a chair: they greeted each the other friendly, and then Hedinn told her of his deeds, and thereof was she well content. She had with her the horn whereof he had drunk afore, and again she bade him drink thereof; so he took it and drank, and when he had drunk sleep came upon him, and he fell tottering into her lap: but when he slept she drew away from his head and spake: "Now hallow I thee, and give thee to lie under all those spells and the weird that Odin commanded, thee and Hogni, and all the hosts of you."

Then awoke Hedinn, and saw the ghostly shadow of Gondul, and him-seemed she was waxen black and over big; and all things came to his mind again, and mighty woe he deemed it. And now was he minded to get him far away somewhither, lest he hear daily the blame and shame of his evil deed.

So he went to the ship and they unmoored speedily: the wind blew off shore, and so he sailed away with Hild.

CHAPTER VIII

THE WEIRD FALLETH ON THESE TWAIN, HOGNI AND HEDINN

Now cometh Hogni home, and comes to wot the sooth, that Hedinn hath sailed away with Hild and the dragon Halfdans-loom, and his queen is left dead there. Full wroth was Hogni thereat, and bade men turn about straightway and sail after Hedinn. Even so did they speedily, and they had a wind of the best, and ever came at eve to the haven whence Hedinn had sailed the morning afore.

But on a day whenas Hogni made the haven, lo the sails of Hedinn in sight on the main; so Hogni, he and his, stood after them; and most sooth is it told that a head-wind fell on Hedinn, whiles the same fair wind went with Hogni.

So Hedinn brought-to at an isle called Ha, and lay in the roadstead there, and speedily came Hogni up with him; and when they met Hedinn greeted him softly: "Needs must I say, foster-brother," saith he, "how evil hath befallen me, that none may amend save thou: for I have taken from thee thy daughter and thy dragon; and thy queen I have done to death. And yet is this deed done not from my evil heart alone, but rather from wicked witchcraft and evil spells; and now will I that thou alone shear and shape betwixt us. But I will offer thee to forego both Hild and the dragon, my men and all my wealth, and to fare so far out in the world that I may never come into the Northlands again, or thine eye-sight, whiles I live."

Hogni answered: "I would have given thee Hild, hadst thou wooed her; yea, and though thou hadst borne away Hild from me, yet for all that might we have had peace: but whereas thou hast now wrought a dastard's deed in the laying down of my queen and slaying of her, there is no hope that I may ever take atonement from thee; but here, in this place, shall we try straightway which of us twain hath more skill in the smiting of strokes."

Hedinn answered: "Rede it were, since thou wilt nought else but battle, that we twain try it alone, for no man here is guilty against thee saving I alone: and nowise meet it is that guiltless men should pay for my folly and ill-doing."

But the followers of either of them answered as with one mouth, that they would all fall one upon the other rather than that they two should play alone.

So when Hedinn saw that Hogni would nought else but battle, he bade his men go up a-land: "For I will fail Hogni no longer, nor beg off the battle: so let each do according to his manhood."

So they go up a-land now and fight: full fierce is Hogni, and Hedinn apt at arms and mighty of stroke.

Soothly is it said that such mighty and evil spells went with the weird of these, that though they clave each other down to the shoulders, yet still they stood upon their feet and fought on and ever sat Hild in a grove and looked on the play.

So this travail and torment went on ever from the time they first fell a-fighting till the time that Olaf Tryggvison was king in Norway; and men say that it was an hundred and forty and three years before the noble man, King

Olaf, brought it so about that his courtman loosed them from this woeful labour and miserable grief of heart.

CHAPTER IX

HOGNI AND HEDINN ARE
LOOSED FROM THEIR WEIRD

So tells the tale, that in the first year of the reign of King Olaf he came to the Isle of Ha, and lay in the haven there on an eve. Now such was the way of things in that isle, that every night whoso watched there vanished away, so that none knew what was become of them.

On this night had Ivar Gleam-bright to hold ward: so when all on ship-board were asleep Ivar took his sword, which Iron-shield of Heathwood had owned erst, and Thorstein his son had given to Ivar, and all his war-gear he took withal, and so went up on to the isle.

But when he was gotten up there, lo a man coming to meet him, great of growth, and all bloody, and exceeding sorrowful of countenance. Ivar asked that man of his name; and he said he was called Hedinn, the son of Hiarandi, of the blood of Serkland.

"Sooth have I to tell thee," said he, "that whereas the watchmen have vanished away, ye must lay it to me and to Hogni, the son of Halfdan; for we and our men are fallen under such sore weird and labour, that we fight on both night and day; and so hath it been with us for many generations of men; and Hild, the daughter of Hogni, sitteth by and looketh on. Odin hath laid this weird upon us, nor shall aught loose us therefrom till a christened man fight with us; and then whoso he smiteth down shall rise up no more; and in such wise shall each one of us be loosed from his labour. Now will I crave of thee to go with me to the battle, for I wot that thou art well christened; and thy king also whom thou servest is of great goodhap, of whom my heart telleth me, that of him and his men shall we have somewhat good."

Ivar said yea to going with him; and glad was Hedinn thereat, and said: "Be thou ware not to meet Hogni face to face, and again that thou slay not me before him; for no mortal man may look Hogni in the face, or slay him if I be dead first: for he hath the Aegis-helm in the eyes of him, nor may any shield him thence. So there is but one thing for it, that I face him and fight him, whilst thou goest at his back and so givest him his death-blow; for it will be but easy work for thee to slay me, though I be left alive the longest of us all."

Therewith went they to the battle, and Ivar seeth that all is sooth that Hedinn hath told him: so he goeth to the back of Hogni, and smiteth him into his head, and cleaveth him down to the shoulders: and Hogni fell dead, and never rose up again.

Then slew Ivar all those men who were at the battle, and Hedinn last of all, and that was no hard work for him. But when he came to the grove wherein Hild was wont to sit, lo she was vanished away.

Then went Ivar to the ship, when it was now daybreak, and he came to the king and told him hereof: and the king made much of his deed, and said that it had gone luckily with him.

But the next day they went a-land, and thither where the battle had been, and saw nowhere any signs of what had befallen there: but blood was seen on Ivar's sword as a token thereof; and never after did the watchmen vanish away.

So after these things the king went back to his realm.

The End of This Tale